The Grandma Cure

by **PAMELA MAYER**   illustrated by **JOHN NEZ**

DUTTON CHILDREN'S BOOKS · NEW YORK

For my sweet Rebecca
P.M.

For Ann, Arthur & Evan
and their Grandmas Marija & Maryann
J.N.

DUTTON CHILDREN'S BOOKS
A division of Penguin Young Readers Group
Published by the Penguin Group
Penguin Group (USA) Inc., 375 Hudson Street, New York, New York 10014, U.S.A.
Penguin Group (Canada), 10 Alcorn Avenue, Toronto, Ontario, Canada M4V 3B2 (a division of Pearson Penguin Canada Inc.)
Penguin Books Ltd, 80 Strand, London WC2R 0RL, England
Penguin Ireland, 25 St Stephen's Green, Dublin 2, Ireland (a division of Penguin Books Ltd)
Penguin Group (Australia), 250 Camberwell Road, Camberwell, Victoria 3124, Australia (a division of Pearson Australia Group Pty Ltd)
Penguin Books India Pvt Ltd, 11 Community Centre, Panchsheel Park, New Delhi - 110 017, India
Penguin Group (NZ), Cnr Airborne and Rosedale Roads, Albany, Auckland 1310, New Zealand (a division of Pearson New Zealand Ltd)
Penguin Books (South Africa) (Pty) Ltd, 24 Sturdee Avenue, Rosebank, Johannesburg 2196, South Africa
Penguin Books Ltd, Registered Offices: 80 Strand, London WC2R 0RL, England

Library of Congress Cataloging-in-Publication Data
Mayer, Pamela.
The Grandma Cure / by Pamela Mayer; illustrated by John Nez.—1st ed.
p. cm.
Summary: When her grandmothers disagree over how to take care of her while she has a cold, Becky is reminded of the behavior
of her kindergarten classmates and instructs them as her teacher would to take their seats, take turns, and share.
ISBN 0-525-47559-1
[1. Grandmothers—Fiction. 2. Behavior—Fiction. 3. Sick—Fiction.] I. Title: The Grandma Cure. II. Nez, John A., ill. III. Title.
PZ7.M463Gr 2005 [E]—dc22 2004056182

Published in the United States by Dutton Children's Books,
a division of Penguin Young Readers Group
345 Hudson Street, New York, New York 10014
www.penguin.com/youngreaders

Designed by Gloria Cheng and Tim Hall

Manufactured in China · First Edition
1 3 5 7 9 10 8 6 4 2

When Becky caught a cold and had to stay home from kindergarten,
Mommy telephoned Becky's grandmas.

"Orange juice and chicken-noodle soup,"
Grandma Sophie said. "I'll be right over!"
She carried a jar of each in a shopping bag.

Grandma Sophie took Becky's temperature, plumped her pillows, and held her hand tight when she had to drink the yucky-tasting medicine.

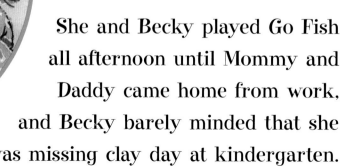

She and Becky played Go Fish all afternoon until Mommy and Daddy came home from work, and Becky barely minded that she was missing clay day at kindergarten.

The next morning, Grandma Rosalie came.

"Hot tea with lemon and rice pudding," Grandma Rosalie said.

"I'm on my way!"

She put the kettle on to boil as soon as she arrived at Becky's house.

Grandma Rosalie tucked in Becky's covers, put a cold compress on her hot forehead, and held her hand tight when she had to drink the yucky-tasting medicine.

She read picture books to Becky all afternoon, and it hardly mattered that today was finger-painting day at kindergarten.

The next day, Becky still had a cold. Grandma Sophie came again.

And so did Grandma Rosalie.

Becky thought her grandmas
acted as if two were one too many,
so she asked, "Can you both stay?"
The grandmas hurried up the
stairs so fast they nearly collided.

Grandma Sophie plumped Becky's pillows while
Grandma Rosalie tucked in her covers.

They both wanted to be the one to sit at the foot of Becky's bed.

They reminded Becky of her kindergarten class before everyone settled down in the morning.

She told her grandmas what Ms. Chu always told them:

"All present!"

Please take your seats!"

Then Grandma Sophie pulled a
chair up to the right side of Becky's bed,
and Grandma Rosalie pulled one up to the left.

Becky sneezed. Twice.

"Gesundheit!"

"Bless you!"

Grandma Sophie handed Becky a tissue.
Grandma Rosalie pulled out a lace handkerchief.

Then Grandma Sophie ran downstairs to squeeze oranges,
and Grandma Rosalie hurried to put on the kettle.
"Drink this, darling," Grandma Sophie said.
"Orange juice is very good for a cold."
"I stirred both lemon and honey into your tea today, sweetheart,"
Grandma Rosalie said. "Nothing beats a hot drink."

"Orange juice is the best!"

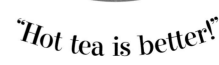

"Hot tea is better!"

They reminded Becky of Amy and Clarissa when they fought about who would be the first one down the slide.

She told her grandmas what Ms. Chu always told them:

"Take turns, please!"

Then Becky drank the orange juice,
and when she was finished, she drank the tea.

Becky coughed. Both grandmas ran to the medicine cabinet.

"It's time to take the yucky-tasting medicine, dearhearty," Grandma Sophie called.

"I'll hold your hand, sweetpea," Grandma Rosalie said.

"I want to hold Becky's hand!" Grandma Sophie said.
"You give her the yucky-tasting medicine. I'll hold her hand!"
Grandma Rosalie said.

"I am holding Becky's hand!"

"No, I am!"

"Me!"

"ME!"

Her grandmas reminded Becky of Jeffrey when he tried to grab all the blocks away from Sam, so Becky told them what Ms. Chu always told him:

"Remember to share!"

Then Becky swallowed the yucky-tasting medicine all by herself,
and when she was finished, she held hands with each of her grandmas.
"Grandmas," Becky warned, "if you don't behave,
I will have to separate you."

They tried to be good, but when lunchtime came, Grandma Rosalie shouted, "My delicious rice pudding!"

And Grandma Sophie cried, "My nutritious chicken-noodle soup!"

"Rice pudding is very good when someone is sick," Grandma Rosalie told Grandma Sophie.

"And I suppose soup isn't?" Grandma Sophie asked.

The grandmas glared at each other. Grandma Sophie rolled her eyes, and Grandma Rosalie stuck out her tongue.

Then Grandma Sophie lay down on the floor and kicked her feet.

"Rice pudding! Rice pudding!"

"My nutritious chicken soup!"

Grandma Rosalie jumped up and down and waved her arms.

They reminded Becky of the first day of kindergarten class before anyone knew the rules.

She threw back the covers and stood up on her bed.

"GRANDMAS!

You are acting like you are still in preschool!"

Then she sat her grandmas down for circle time,
and for the next hour she taught them all
the useful things that Ms. Chu had taught her.

When she was finished teaching, Becky asked,
"Are we ready for lunchtime now?"
Grandma Sophie and Grandma Rosalie
walked downstairs in a straight line.

They took turns in the kitchen
and remembered to share the tray
when they brought Becky her lunch.

Grandma Sophie raised her hand.

"Soup and pudding are very nice together," she said.

Grandma Rosalie passed out the napkins. She was paper monitor.

Becky ate up all of her chicken-noodle soup
and all of her rice pudding.

They did such a good job that Becky made
Grandma S. Citizen of the Day and
Grandma R. Special Helper of the Day.
She told her grandmas what
Ms. Chu always told the class:

"I am very proud of you!"

For the rest of the afternoon, Becky and her grandmas played
Go Fish and read picture books and drew pictures and cut out
paper dolls, and it was as much fun as kindergarten.

The next day, Becky was so much better, she went back to school. And Grandma Sophie and Grandma Rosalie went out to lunch together— to practice what they had learned.